Bad Dog Bonnie

Books About Bonnie:

Big Dog Bonnie • Best Dog Bonnie

Bad Dog Bonnie • Brave Dog Bonnie

Busy Dog Bonnie • Bright Dog Bonnie

Bad Dog Bonnie

BEL MOONEY

Illustrated by Sarah McMenemy

WALKER
BOOKS

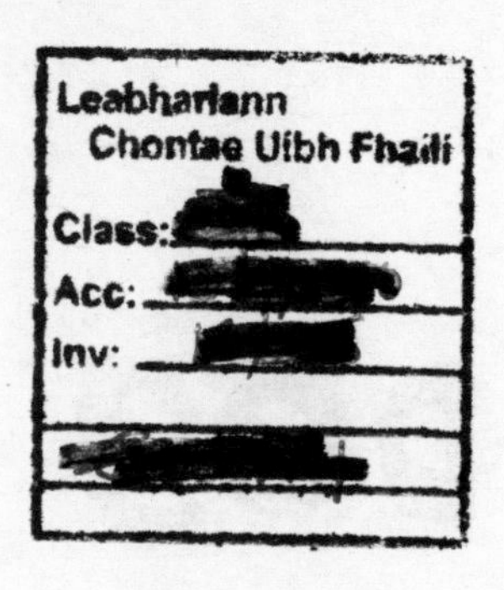

This is a work of fiction. Names, characters, places and incidents are either the product of the author's imagination or, if real, used fictitiously.

First published 2008 by Walker Books Ltd
87 Vauxhall Walk, London SE11 5HJ

This edition published 2013

2 4 6 8 10 9 7 5 3 1

This book has been typeset in StempelSchneidler

Printed and bound in Great Britain by Clays Ltd, St Ives plc

British Library Cataloguing in Publication Data:
a catalogue record for this book is available from the British Library

ISBN 978-1-4063-5115-6

www.walker.co.uk

For Isabella and Max Meikle

B.M.

For my father, James

S.M.

Trouble

Harry was never late for school. He hated fuss; it made him nervous. He had the kind of mum who worried about things just a bit too much, so it made sense to keep her happy and fuss-free. Ever since Bonnie had come to live with them, she'd been much more relaxed; but still, you couldn't be too careful. Zack, his friend next door, always said that when mums blow up, well ... even volcanoes get scared.

As usual Harry woke to feel Bonnie cuddling up to him, but there was no time to waste. He jumped up, went to the bathroom, called to Mum that yes, he'd love a boiled egg, then ran back to his bedroom to dress. There was Bonnie sitting on his bedside rug, as good as gold.

It didn't take long to put on his school uniform, but then...

"Where's my other shoe?" he muttered, looking around. "I know I left them both by the wardrobe last night."

One black shoe stood where he had left it, but it was very lonely.

He searched all around the wardrobe, under his desk, behind the curtains, in every corner – but found no shoe. Then he got on his stomach to peer under the bed, where he found lots of fluff, a biro, three odd socks, a pencil sharpener, two dog biscuits and a plastic toy that had come free in his cereal – but no shoe.

Yip, said Bonnie, darting forward to investigate the plastic toy. Then she ran round in circles, pretending to attack his shoeless foot. "I haven't got time to play," whispered Harry. "Mum'll be here in a second."

And sure enough, she was. "Your egg's ready," she began. Then: "Oh, Harry, why haven't you got your shoes on yet?"

"I started!" he said, pointing to one foot.

Tutting, she searched, just as he had. Then she gave a short, sharp sigh. "Where did you last have that shoe, Harry?"

"On my foot!" he replied.

She didn't think it was funny, but Bonnie seemed to smile.

Mum glanced at her watch and gave a little cry. "Look at the time! Get your bag; you'll have to go to school in your trainers."

"But we're not allowed..." he began – then he saw her face and decided he'd better do as she said.

He rushed into the living room to look for his bag, started to push his homework into it, dropped a book, bent to pick it up – and spotted the missing shoe.

There it was, nestled in Bonnie's squishy little bed.

Uh-oh, he thought, *Bonnie will be in trouble again!* He had to save her.

Just lately the little dog kept getting into scrapes. There was the Case of the Missing Phone Bill, for example. One day Mum had a call from the telephone company reminding her she hadn't paid her bill.

"What bill?" she squeaked indignantly.

They found it torn to pieces under Harry's bed.

"You're a mischievous dog!" frowned Mum, wagging her finger at Bonnie.

Who wagged her tail right back.

Then there was the Case of the Smelly Sausage. Harry loved sausages, mash and baked beans, and he quickly discovered that Bonnie did too. Mum forbade him to feed Bonnie titbits from the table, but one evening she didn't notice he had Bonnie on his knee when she put his plate in front of him.

She went to answer the phone and Harry began to daydream, wondering if the call was from Dad (who promised to ring every Wednesday but sometimes forgot) – and next thing he knew, there were two sausages instead of three on his plate, and Bonnie had vanished.

Harry started to eat quickly, not wanting Mum to see what had happened. Seconds later, Bonnie appeared at the kitchen door. Was she licking her lips? Her tiny mouth couldn't possibly have finished off a whole sausage in that time…

Harry searched, but there was no sign of the missing sausage. Not until about a week later, when Mum suddenly sniffed the air.

"What's that funny smell?" It was pretty bad; and as the hours passed, it got worse. It seemed to be coming from the sofa, so Mum took off all the cushions, but found nothing.

"What have you done, Bonnie?" she asked sternly.

Bonnie sniffed the air too and looked worried.

"But, Mum, it's not *that* kind of smell," Harry protested. They'd put a cat flap in the back door so Bonnie could go in the garden when she needed to.

In the end Mum couldn't bear it any longer. She pulled the sofa out, and there it was: a rotting sausage.

"Oh, gross!" said Harry.

When he explained, Mum tried not to smile. "I can't blame the dog," she said. "In a way it's your fault for having her on your knee when you're not supposed to. But she really is Trouble these days."

But the worst crime Bonnie had committed was the Case of the Fallen Cyclist. That day, Mum got cross. Very cross indeed. It all started when they came back from the park, where Bonnie had not behaved well – pulling on the long extending lead and barking so fiercely at much bigger dogs that Harry had warned, "You'll get eaten one day."

They were
just walking past
Zack and Zena's house,
when a tabby cat came out of
nowhere and darted in front of them.
Bonnie yipped and yapped, and took off
after it, the lead skittering along the
pavement behind her.

"Bonnie, come here!" shouted Harry.

"Stop, Bonnie, stop!" yelled Mum.

But the little dog took no notice. Terrified she'd run into the road, Harry shot off after her, but Bonnie was so fast!

Zack and Zena called
her Pocket Rocket or Racing Rabbit
because, once she started to run,
you just couldn't catch her.

Coming towards them was a teenage girl pushing a bicycle. She wore very smart sports gear and was obviously carried away listening to her iPod, noticing nothing.

It was all over in seconds. The cat suddenly swerved to one side and scampered halfway up a tree. Bonnie followed – right in front of the bicycle. The trailing lead got tangled in the front wheel and the bike keeled over. The girl tried to save herself, but she was too late. Over she went too, landing in a pile on the pavement with her bike and the dog.

"Oh, I'm so sorry!" Mum cried, rushing up to help her.

"Ow!" moaned the girl, rubbing her knee. She looked very bad-tempered as Mum fussed around her.

"Look at the state of my new tracksuit!" she whinged, flapping her hand at the dirt all over her bright pink jogging bottoms (Harry thought it was funny how her face changed colour to match). Eventually she went on her way, muttering complaints about stupid little dogs that got out of control. Harry and his mum went into their flat in silence, Bonnie trotting meekly behind on her lead.

"She's a very disobedient dog," said Mum.

"No, she's not," Harry protested. "All dogs chase cats. It's what they do."

"You can't make excuses for her this time, Harry," Mum snapped. "All good dogs come when they're called – simple as that! Something will have to be done."

And now here was Bonnie a week later: guilty of the Case of the Stolen Shoe!

Harry knew he had to grab the shoe before Mum saw where it was. But he was too late. She swept into the living room just as he was retrieving it from Bonnie's bed.

"Oops!" was all he could say, smiling down at the little dog. "Think we might be in trouble again, Bons."

Bonnie jumped as Mum clapped her hands sharply.

"That bad dog!" she said, all in a fluster. "Now she's made you late for school."

Bonnie's head and tail both drooped low.

As a punishment she wasn't allowed to walk to school with them, but by that evening Mum seemed to have forgotten about the shoe incident. She helped Harry with his project on the Romans, then they watched TV, Bonnie snuggled happily between them on the sofa.

At last Harry couldn't keep quiet any more. "Do you really think Bonnie's naughty?" he asked.

"Well, yes," said Mum, "I'm afraid I do."

"But how can a dog be called naughty when she doesn't know any different?"

"She understands the word *no*," said Mum, "but then she does it anyway."

"Are you naughty, Bonnie?" Harry asked.

Bonnie put her head on one side. Her pink tongue lolled out, and Harry got the giggles. "Look, she's sticking her tongue out at me!" he laughed.

So Harry stuck his tongue out at Bonnie, who ran across the room and took a flying leap onto the armchair – where Harry had dumped his school bag. It fell to the ground, and all of Harry's work slipped out.

Including his precious project folder.

Including the beautiful drawing of a Roman centurion which had taken him so long.

Before they could get there, Bonnie had seized it in her teeth, growling and shaking it to and fro.

"NO!" yelled Mum.

"Drop it!" shouted Harry, leaping forward to try to rescue the picture.

Too late.

He looked sadly at his tattered drawing, but for Bonnie's sake tried to hide his feelings.

"Well, Mum," he said with a little lopsided grin, "d'you reckon my teacher will believe the dog really did eat my homework?"

BONNIE was puzzled.

Sometimes you didn't know where you were with people. Why was Harry's mum always barking at her? She used to make those cooing noises, especially when she was coming at her with a brush and comb, but just lately it had been bark, bark, bark. And what about Harry? He used to love playing with her, waving bits of paper for her to jump up and bite. "Kill it!" he would cry when she shook the paper to and fro.

But now it was wrong. How was a dog to know what to do? And how could she make him understand that she only took his shoe because it smelled just like him?

After all, a dog always has her reasons for making mischief.

So Naughty

"What are we going to do about Bonnie's behaviour?" became a question Mum asked every few days. Harry tried to explain that now Bonnie had got used to living with them, and was growing (in age if not in size), she was bound to spread her wings a bit.

"Harry, she's a dog, not a bird," said Mum.

"You know what I mean!" Harry protested. Then he giggled. "Mind you, if Bonnie had wings she'd be a little angel, wouldn't she?"

"All in white too!" laughed Mum. But then her face became all serious again. "But she can be so naughty, Harry! She chased the Wilsons' chickens, and I don't think those birds have ever got over it."

Next door, Zack and Zena's parents had decided to keep two chickens in their garden, so the family could enjoy fresh, organic eggs. They'd bought a bright pink chickenhouse called an Eglu and Zack and Zena called their new pets Egg and Chips – which made Harry laugh for ages.

But just four weeks after the chickens had started supplying delicious eggs for the twins' breakfast, the terrible thing happened.

Bonnie hadn't met the chickens yet, although Harry had seen her sitting near to the fence, listening curiously to the gentle "cluck-cluck-cluck" sounds from next door.

One day Zena asked him to bring Bonnie round so she could play with her. "She hasn't been to our house for ages," she said.

So Harry took Bonnie visiting – and of course, she disgraced herself. Mrs Wilson was just pouring them all some juice in the kitchen, when Bonnie saw that the back door was open. She wandered into the garden, planning to bark at that stupid rabbit called Major, who thought he was so tough because he was bigger than her, but who hid at the back of his cage when he heard her yip!

And there, wandering about freely out of their run, were the chickens.

What fun! Yelping like mad, Bonnie made a dash at the first one, who squawked and fluttered up into a low tree in a panic.

"Bonnie – come here!" shouted Harry, tearing out into the garden, followed by Zena and Zack. But the dog was off in pursuit of the second bird, who fled in terror – straight back into the chicken run. Naturally Bonnie followed. Into the safe pink house ran the chicken – and Bonnie was just about to dive inside after her, when Harry arrived and yelled at the top of his voice for her to stop.

"You're a bad dog!" he shouted.

"Poor Egg and Chips," said Zack, "they've never seen a Wild Wabbit before."

Tail between her legs, Bonnie slunk out of the chicken run and sat down in front of Harry. She looked up as if to plead, "But what have I done wrong?"

Chips stayed up in the tree for the rest of the day and wouldn't come down, while Egg was too terrified to leave the chickenhouse.

Next morning both birds were rootling about on the lawn as usual, but when Zack went to collect breakfast the special little egg place was empty.

"It's not really Bonnie's fault," said Zena kindly. "She just wanted to play with Egg and Chips, that's all."

"How d'you know she didn't want to *eat* egg and chips?" joked Zack.

Even though the chickens soon started laying again, Harry felt awful. How was he ever going to calm Mum down when Bonnie kept causing so much trouble?

Little did he know, but his task was about to get harder than ever.

It was the Postman Incident that finally did it for Mum. They had a friendly, cheerful postman called Alan, who always seemed to be smiling, even when the rain was pouring down. If ever he had to ring the doorbell because something was too big for the letter box, Bonnie would dart out and seize the bottom of his trousers, pulling and growling.

"Kill!" Harry would cry.

"Oh, *nooo* – I'm *so* scared of the giant hound!" Alan would say, collapsing with laughter.

One Saturday morning they heard the doorbell ring, and Harry and Mum raced each other. She was waiting for a new dress she'd ordered from a catalogue; Harry was expecting a letter and a magazine from his father, who lived in London.

"Yip yip yip yip YIP!" went Bonnie's ear-splitting battle cry.

When Mum opened the door, Bonnie tore out as usual, yapping and growling all at once, looking for those familiar blue trousers. But today it wasn't Alan, and there were no trousers.

This postman was older than Alan, and had a mean face. Worse, because it was a warm day, he was wearing shorts. It took just a few seconds for Bonnie to dart around his trainers and socks, feel puzzled, look up, see the shorts – and launch herself into the air to try to bite these exciting new trousers.

Bonnie was famous for her leaps. She could take off from standing and land on the sofa so quickly that Harry sometimes called her Chopper Dog. But this time there was nothing to land on. She just about reached the bottom of the dark blue shorts, then fell back, scrabbling wildly with her front paws and…

"Ow! It scratched me!" roared the postman.

"Grrrrr," snarled Bonnie, crouching low.

"Oh, I'm *so* sorry," said Mum.

"I should think you are!" grunted the postman, rubbing his leg. "That really hurt!"

Harry peered at the long white scratch marks and tried not to laugh. Silly man, making such a fuss, he thought, but he bent to pick up his pet and tried to look sorry.

"You need to keep that animal under control," said the postman, handing over letters and a parcel.

"I'm so sorry," said Mum again.

"I could make a complaint, you know," he added with a sniff. "When a bloke's doing his job, he doesn't expect to be bitten."

Harry couldn't stand it any more. "She didn't bite you!" he cried out. "Where's the blood? I mean, a little scratch never hurt anybody."

"Harry!" cried Mum.

"He's just a wimp and a wuss and a weed!" said Harry defiantly.

"Is that a fact? Well, you haven't heard the last of this," warned the postman, and stomped away down the garden path.

Sure enough, three days later a letter arrived from the post office manager.

It informed them that a complaint had been made and that if they didn't keep their dog under control, there would be serious consequences.

"Aargh!" cried Harry.

He and Mum had done some research on the Internet and discovered that in the very worst cases a dangerous dog could be put to sleep. It had happened more than once when postmen had been bitten.

"They can't do that to Bons, can they, Mum?" asked Harry miserably.

"Of course not, love – but she'd better learn how to behave. She can't go on being so naughty."

The doorbell rang and Bonnie did her usual thing – which was to take a flying leap from wherever she was sitting, scrabble to get her balance, tear to the front door then spin round in circles on the doormat, before hurling herself at the door, yelping and scratching at the paintwork.

"Better grab hold of her in case it's the postman," sighed Mum. "I wish Alan would come back from his holidays!"

But there at the door stood Zack and Zena, holding a flat, square parcel neatly wrapped in newspaper.

"Special delivery!" they chorused.

"We're worried about Bonnie getting into scrapes," explained Zena.

"No, we're worried about that postman getting scraped!" laughed Zack.

"So we've made you this," said Zena.

They handed Harry the parcel. He unwrapped it to find a large wooden board with the words BEWARE OF THE DOG painted on it in wobbly red letters.

"If you put it up out the front, the postman can't say there isn't a warning, you see," Zack explained. "It's what you're supposed to do."

"We nearly put 'Beware of the Rabbit'," Zena smiled.

Harry didn't know whether to laugh or cry, but Mum was delighted. She grabbed the sign. "That's such a brilliant idea, kids! Pure genius! I'm going to put it on the gate right now."

When the doorbell rang the following Saturday, Mum opened the door to find Alan outside, helpless with laughter.

"No parcel … today … folks," he spluttered. "I just had to … ask you … what's … what's this?" He put down his bag and pointed at the sign. "You telling me I have to beware of a … a … powder puff? Ha ha ha HA HA…"

As soon as Alan had wiped away his tears of laughter, Mum explained and he nodded. He'd heard the rumour that the unpopular new postman had complained about Bonnie.

"All the lads think he's a joke," he went on. "And talking of jokes, Harry, I wish you'd put her down so she can terrify my trousers!"

"Grrrrrr," said Bonnie, as Harry obliged.

🐾 🐾 🐾

That afternoon they went to the park to meet their new friend Olga, whom Harry had decided to make his honorary gran. Olga listened as Mum told her all about Bonnie's misdeeds, and once or twice she looked as if she was trying hard not to laugh.

"The truth is, Bonnie doesn't know what *naughty* means," said Olga when the saga was finished.

"That's what I said!" crowed Harry.

"Yes, but she could still do with some training," Olga went on. "Did you know there are special schools for dogs?"

Harry looked at Mum and Mum looked at Harry.

"School? Of course!" said Mum. "That's the answer!"

"School?" echoed Harry a little less enthusiastically. "Maybe Bonnie will get to say the boy ate *her* homework!"

BONNIE sat at the edge of the path, watching them talk. The funny old lady who needed grooming was looking at her and smiling. What was it now? Harry and his mum both seemed as worried as ever. What was wrong with her pack these days?

Why hadn't they understood that she was protecting them from that man with the cross face and the silly short trousers? You had to be careful with strangers.

Grrrrrr, she'd told him, and *grrrrrr* was what she'd tell anybody who couldn't be trusted. Harry was the sweetest, kindest puppy in the whole world, and Bonnie knew her job was to look after him.

Even if that sometimes meant she got into trouble.

Problem Dog

"Good morning, and welcome to the Best-Ever Dog Intensive One-Day Training Course," said the man in the green bow tie. "And the first thing I'm going to say is this: it is *absolutely* vital for you all to realize that sometimes it's a dog's owner who needs training." He had one of those voices which said, I am much cleverer than all of you, and I hope you realize it.

"You see, the first rule of dog training is that a dog can only be as good as his or her owner. When a dog is disobedient we may blame the animal, but we should be blaming ourselves."

(Oh no! thought Harry. Why does everybody try to make me feel guilty? I mean, if Bonnie does a poo on the path instead of the grass, is that supposed to be my fault?)

The man was still talking. "We can only do some basics in one day, but I hope this will encourage you to take our one-week course..."

(A whole week of listening to him? No way! thought Harry.)

"...at the end of which we guarantee to have turned your canine companions into good citizens."

"What?" muttered Harry under his breath.

He couldn't take his eyes off that bow tie. Then he surveyed the shiny brown brogues, neatly pressed beige trousers, green tweed jacket and cream checked shirt, all topped off with an elegant quiff of white hair – and wondered what on earth a man like that was doing training dogs. He looked much too tidy.

Which was more than you could say for the motley collection of mutts lined up in front of him. There was a cheeky-looking mongrel with black patches on his back, a very raggy Border collie, a sleek springer spaniel, a rather fat and slobbery labrador and last – and definitely least as far as Harry was concerned – a minuscule chihuahua, which made Bonnie seem positively huge. As for Bonnie herself, she looked quite scruffy again. Mum had tried to brush her hair ready for school, but she'd wriggled and

tried to attack the brush so much that Mum had given up with a sigh.

"I was going to come with you, Harry, but I can feel one of my headaches coming on. Anyway, it's much better if just one of us takes control of Bonnie."

Harry was about to point out that *she* was the one who'd gone to the Cats' and Dogs' Home behind his back and brought home the very opposite of the kind of dog he'd always dreamed of, so *she* really ought to take responsibility… But then he looked down and caught Bonnie gazing at him with such a sweet face that he changed his mind. "Come to school with me, Harry," she seemed to be pleading. "The other dogs might pick on me."

"Yes," Harry decided, "I'm the best one to look after Bonnie." Besides, he thought, I might learn a few things myself.

Bonnie was already pulling on her lead, while the other dogs sat quiet and still, all of them looking rather shell-shocked, as if wondering what was going on. The man in the bow tie was called Mr Catskill, which made Harry want to giggle. Surely he should be training cats not dogs!

"And now I think we should all introduce ourselves," Mr Catskill instructed.

The mongrel was with a teenage boy, who slouched and muttered so they could hardly hear him say, "I'm Jake … an' he's Spotty."

(So are you! thought Harry.)

The Border collie, whose black hair ran into the white, sat at the feet of a middle-aged lady with short, shaggy grey hair.

"My name is Ellen, and this is Sam," she said enthusiastically.

(And you and your dog have the same hairstyle! thought Harry.)

The springer spaniel pulled at an elegant leopard-print lead which matched the handbag and belt of the tall young woman in jeans and high-heeled boots. "My dog's called Mitch and I'm Mimi," she trilled.

(Is your dog just a fashion accessory? wondered Harry.)

The Labrador sat meekly at the feet of a plump, elderly man with a shiny bald head and a gentle face.

"This is Ben, and he eats too much," he said earnestly, "and – you know how it is – I suppose I'm too soft to say no..."

"That's the first word a dog must learn," said Mr Catskill crisply, "and you haven't told us your name, sir!"

"Oh, I'm sorry. It's William, but, er, everybody calls me Bill." (Poor Bill and Ben! thought Harry.)

Next in line was the chihuahua, a pale dog at the end of a bright pink lead and collar. Harry had been pleased to see its owner was his age – especially as the blonde girl was so pretty.

"I'm Susie and my dog is called Princess Daisy," she said shyly.

(Oh yuck. *Double yuck*, thought Harry.)

There was a silence, then Harry realized everybody was looking at him. He felt his face go red.

"Oh, yeah – I'm Haz and this is Bons," he mumbled.

Mr Catskill consulted his clipboard. "Really? I have you down here as Harry Smith, accompanied by Bonnie the Maltese," he said in a sniffy voice. "So, Harry, perhaps you could start us off by describing your dog's behaviour, to see if we can find some common ground."

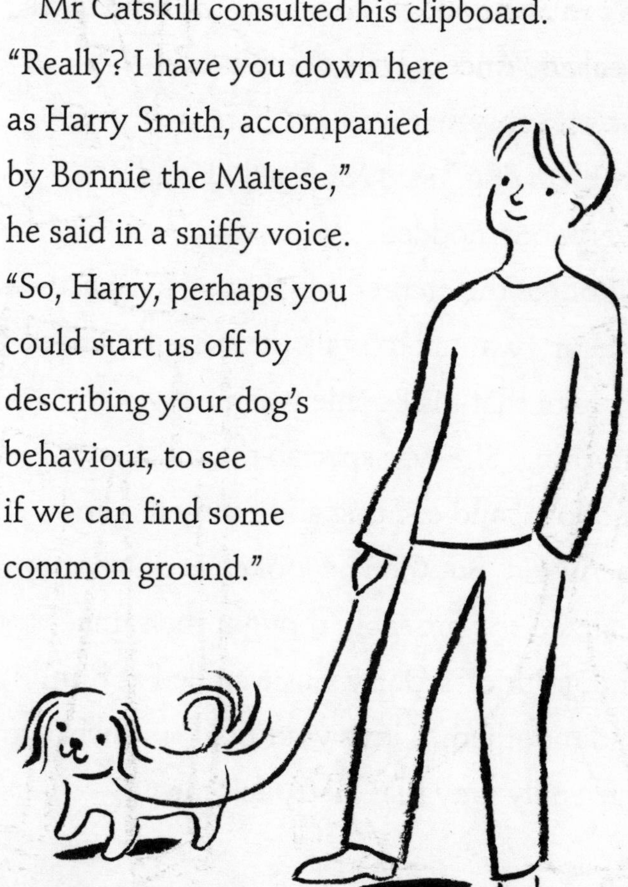

Bonnie looked up at Harry, as if to say, "Don't tell tales on me!" – but what else could he do?

"She … um … won't do what she's told, like sitting and staying and stopping. And she hides things. And tears things up. She yaps at other dogs. And bites the postman's trousers. And … oh, I don't know…"

"Oh yes, what we have here is a *typical* problem dog," said Mr Catskill, and everybody nodded.

Bonnie the arch-criminal hung her head.

Harry wanted to walk out, shouting back at them that his Bonnie wasn't a *typical* anything. She was special: the most loving and loyal and exciting and funny dog in the world. But then he looked at Susie and realized she probably thought the same about Princess Daisy. Susie smiled at him, and mouthed, "I love your dog!" in such a friendly way that Harry felt mean.

Why couldn't he say the same back to her?

But there was no time to waste. Mr Catskill was giving orders. They'd been told to bring healthy dog treats in their pockets, and now they had to position their pets in a line, give the instruction Stay! – then walk to a spot the teacher pointed out, about ten metres away.

"Count to ten, then call, 'Come here!'" said Mr Catskill.

It was chaos. All the dogs got up and followed their owners, except Spotty, who ran off in the opposite direction. And except Bonnie, who sat quivering, her coal-black eyes fixed on Harry. He counted to ten as quickly as he could, then called, "Bonnie, come here!" She tore across the room to him – and all the other dogs and their owners looked impressed.

Harry stared at Bonnie in amazement. What had got into her?

"Well done, Mouse-Face!" he whispered.

"Gosh, your dog's *so* obedient," gushed Susie, nestling Princess Daisy under her arm.

"Nice one, mate," said Jake, watching Spotty leap up and bark at the big, soft Labrador, who was far too lazy to be alarmed.

Mr Catskill's voice cut through the racket. Everybody had to go back and do it again. And again. And again. In the end all the dogs more or less got the hang of sitting and staying, and were rewarded with tasty treats; but each time, Bonnie performed best of all.

"The tone of voice must always be the same for commands," said Mr Catskill. "Dogs need to know exactly where they are."

The next lesson was walking to heel, and that took twice as long. Spotty didn't want to know, Sam ran in circles trying to round up imaginary sheep, Mitch pranced ahead of Mimi as if saying "Look at me!" and poor old Ben just sat down whenever he could, much to Bill's distress. By now Princess Daisy and Bonnie had made friends and were much more interested in rolling over and over in a play fight than walking to heel. Susie caught Harry's eye and they both started to giggle helplessly.

Mr Catskill clapped his hands. "Dogs and owners, dogs and owners – please!"

To Harry's astonishment the next few hours passed quickly. He enjoyed the friendly competition with Susie – especially as Bonnie beat Princess Daisy hands down.

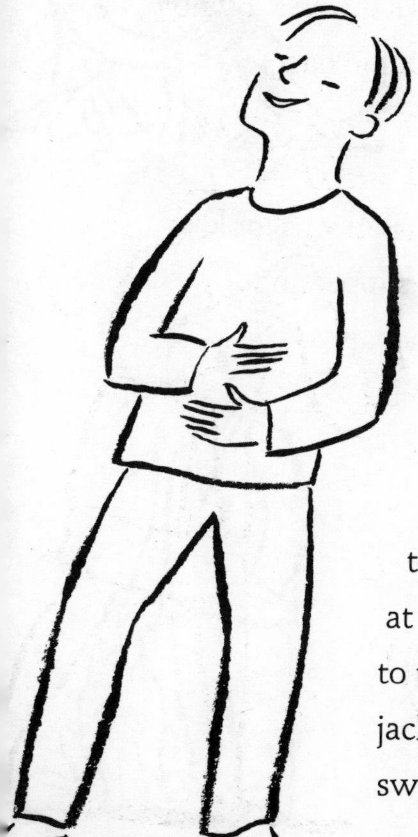

Walking on the lead without pulling, coming to heel, lying down and staying there – they tried it all. Sometimes Harry saw their teacher roll his eyes to the heavens, and at last he was forced to take off his tweed jacket as he wiped sweat from his brow.

Were they really that
stupid? The truth was,
Jake and Spotty just
wanted to hang out
and do nothing
much; Sam wanted to be
fussed over by Ellen;
Mitch wanted
to pose,

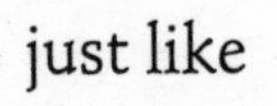

just like
his mistress; Ben was looking
forward to supper and
a nice armchair,
like old Bill;

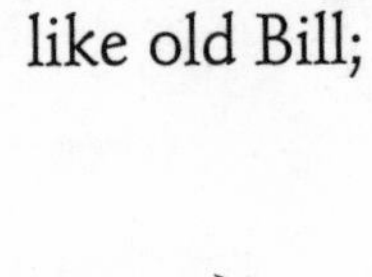

and Princess Daisy thought it was enough to be small and pretty, because then she could get away with anything.

People always said that dogs looked like their owners, but Harry was starting to see that they often acted like them too. He stared down at Bonnie and she seemed to wink back at him. *But what does that say about us, Bons?* he wondered. For a mad moment, Harry saw himself as a small white creature with short legs and a fluffy tail – but it was just too funny.

"What are you laughing at?" asked Susie at his elbow.

"All this," Harry said, waving his hand. "I'm wondering if any of us – including the dogs – will remember any of it tomorrow."

"Tell you what," she said, "why don't we meet up in a week's time to see if Bonnie and Princess Daisy remember? We could have a competition."

"OK," agreed Harry.

It turned out that Susie lived only a short distance from Harry, and she got very excited about making new friends when he told her about Zack and Zena next door.

"If you children would stop talking, your dogs might learn something," boomed Mr Catskill, and the two of them tried to concentrate and set an example to Bonnie and Princess Daisy.

When the class was over, their stern tutor smiled for the first time. "Don't forget, ladies and gentlemen," he beamed, "a well-trained dog is a happy dog."

"And that means you, problem pooch," whispered Harry to Bonnie.

Spotty said goodbye to Sam; Mimi waved an elegant manicured hand at scruffy Ellen; Mitch and Princess Daisy nuzzled each other delicately; Jake ruffled Harry's hair and said, "See ya later"; Susie stroked Ben and told Bill that his dog had the nicest face she'd ever seen – and Bonnie stuck her tongue out at them all, because she knew she was the very best problem dog in the class.

BONNIE was dreaming. A bossy man was telling her what to do, and there were lots of strange dogs around who needed to be taught who was boss.

Oh, she was so busy in her dreams! She chased a chihuahua, barked at a Border collie, sprang at a spaniel, menaced a mongrel, leaped at a Labrador – and then growled at a German shepherd and roared at a Rottweiler and snarled at a St Bernard.

Bring on all the dogs!

Now Harry was waking her, taking her from her soft bed to sit on his lap. He was telling his mum all about the day at dog school, about how Bonnie was the most obedient dog in the class.

"So what changed?" asked Mum. She didn't understand that Bonnie had just been showing off for Harry's sake.

Bonnie hoped that the pretty girl Harry liked would bring Princess Daisy round. It'd make a change to play with someone smaller – someone who knew her place.

It was good being good, Bonnie decided. You got treats and pats and cuddles and more treats.

But if she saw that grumpy old postman again – he'd soon find out what a problem dog was!

Wicked!

How was it, Harry asked himself, that good news could be bad – at the same time? Dad was coming to visit them at their flat at last. That was good. But Mum was upset and uptight about it. That was bad.

He tried not to think too much about the bad times which had led to how they lived now. There was no way he missed all the arguments. No way at all. And that was really good. But he did miss his dad, and that was definitely bad.

Harry lay on his bed, trying to work it all out. As if she knew he felt sad, Bonnie cuddled up to his chest, lifted her face, and licked his neck. He gave her a squeeze, loving that warm doggy smell.

"Just think, Rabbit, some stupid person left you tied to a tree in the park. That was bad. But then you came to live with us – and how good was that?"

She jumped up and licked his face all over till Harry laughed and yelled, "Yuck, yuck – dog lick!"

Dad lived in London now, in a flat with his new girlfriend. Things had been very difficult, and he'd been so long sorting everything out ("Not his fault," said Harry to Mum) that Harry hadn't seen him since before they'd got Bonnie from the Cats' and Dogs' Home. Now he was coming to visit them for the day, to see Harry ("Can't wait, big guy," he said) and to go through some papers with Harry's Mum ("Boring," she sniffed).

"Oh please, Bonnie, don't let them argue," whispered Harry, pulling one of her silky ears through his fingers.

On Saturday morning he waited for the doorbell to ring. Ten o'clock came, then half past, and Mum was just settling that "I-told-you-so" look on her face, when the bell chimed and Bonnie leaped and scampered and whirled and scratched as if a horde of Orcs from *The Lord of the Rings* were on the doorstep and only she could stop them from reaching her family.

Once Dad had released Harry from a hug so tight it brought tears to his eyes, he let out a roar of a laugh. "What's that?" he asked, pointing at Zack and Zena's **BEWARE OF THE DOG** sign. And "What's *that*?" – pointing at the twirling white furball that was growling and chewing at his jeans.

Bonnie crouched down, yipping and yapping.

"She doesn't like strange men," said Mum. "Sensible girl."

"But she'll soon like you, Dad," added Harry quickly.

His dad grinned. "Bit small, isn't she?"

"The best things come small," snapped Mum, "like diamonds."

Harry's dad was tall. Harry took after his mum.

The air in the hall was like frost on a winter window. Harry knew he was talking too much as he led his dad into the living room, jabbering on about how much they liked their flat, his new friends at school, and how great it was to have Zack and Zena living next door. He actually thought he could hear Bonnie encouraging him in his head: *"Yip yip yip, Harry, you're making things all right!"*

Dad put down the bag he was carrying. "Presents!" he called out, and Harry yipped as loudly as his dog. "I know it's not Christmas, mate, but it's been a while, so..."

Out of the bag came new trainers in their box, a football and what Harry had wanted for ages: a mobile phone!

"Brilliant! Thanks, Dad!"

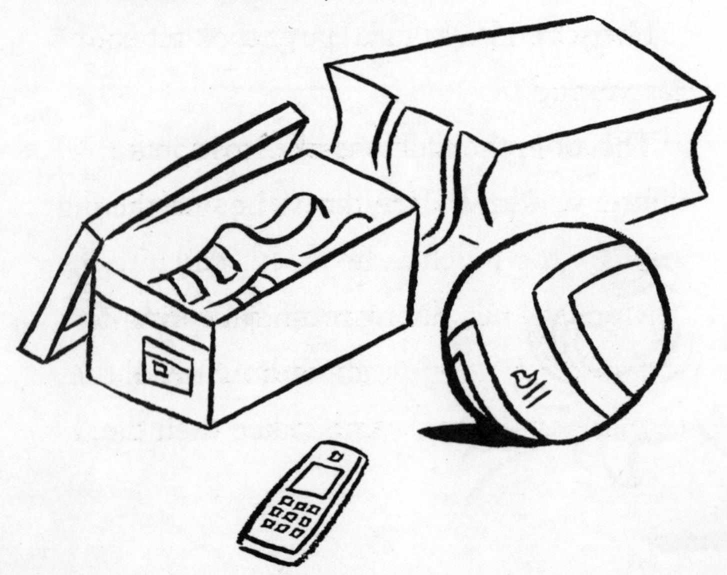

"Great, Dave," muttered Mum. "I hope you'll be forking out for the phone bills."

She plonked herself down on the sofa. Dad took the armchair. Harry looked at the space next to Mum, hesitated, then squatted down on the floor somewhere in the middle. There was an awkward silence. Then Bonnie did one of her amazing flying leaps, landed on the sofa next to Mum, and jumped up to her neck, smothering her with kisses.

"Get down, you silly thing," Mum giggled. But of course, Bonnie couldn't be stopped.

"She seems very keen on you, Ann," said Harry's dad.

"This dog's got good taste, David," she replied, smiling for the first time since he'd arrived.

"Mum rescued her from a life in prison!" explained Harry, and then told the whole story of how Bonnie came to live with them.

Dad made noises of amazement, even though Harry had already told him on the telephone.

"And now she's trained too!" Harry added.

"Really? What tricks can she do? Let's have a demo!"

"This is where you have to be really good, Bonnie," warned Harry, wagging a finger at her. "We want Dad to see how clever you are. Even if you are a bit on the small side."

Harry stood in the centre of the room with the dog. "OK Dad, Bons and me, we went on this one-day intensive course, and she was the best by miles. So – the first lesson was how to sit," he said, and gave the command.

Bonnie just stood there staring at him with her black button eyes, head on one side and pink tongue sticking out.

"Sit!" he repeated, more firmly.

Bonnie didn't move. Harry pressed her rear end down to the ground again and again; but each time, the tail whisked over his hand and the small bottom bounced back up like a yo-yo. It looked very funny.

Dad burst out laughing and Mum couldn't help smiling too.

"OK, so she's not so good at sitting," said Harry.

The next command was "Stay!" – but when Harry uttered that, in his sternest, most commanding voice, Bonnie sauntered into the kitchen to lick her bowl.

Dad threw back his head and let out a huge guffaw. "What an obedient pooch!" he spluttered. "You should be on *Crufts*!"

"Yes, Harry, you've really worked wonders," giggled Mum as Bonnie strolled back into the room, looked around and sat down next to Harry without being told to "sit".

"This dog's got ideas of her own," said Dad.

"Too right!" agreed Mum. "Hey, Harry, what about showing us how she can walk to heel?"

Harry rolled his eyes to heaven. "If this dog was in real school, she'd be at the bottom of the class," he grumbled. Then he felt mean because Bonnie's head and tail seemed to droop.

"Oh, all right," he said. "I'll get the lead."

But as soon as he came back into the room, Bonnie rolled over, waved her paws and snapped at nothing in the air above her.

"I didn't hear you say, 'Roll over'," chortled Dad.

"Maybe he said it in Maltese!" laughed Mum.

Harry felt cross with everybody.

"She wasn't like this at the school. She was top of the class – really she was," he protested. "It must be because you're here, Dad. She's not used to you."

"Oh. I'm sorry for frightening you, Bonnie," said Dad, looking a bit downcast.

But Bonnie ran over and licked the hand he held out to her. She let Dad pick her up, and she sat on his knee without wriggling.

Mum beckoned for Harry to come and sit beside her. "Bonnie doesn't have to obey orders for us to love her, does she, pet?"

"Just as well!" joked Harry's dad.

Their laughter warmed the air. What else could Harry do but join in?

Soon Mum was telling Dad all about Harry's old imaginary dog Prince and how disappointed he was when she first brought Bonnie home.

"No, I wasn't!" he said, glancing nervously at Bonnie. He didn't want her to overhear.

It was so easy to feel small when people kept saying you *were* small.

Bonnie jumped off Dad's knee and came to join Harry on the sofa, curling up on his lap and shutting her eyes.

Mum went on with her stories, launching into tales of Bonnie's misdeeds – especially the Postman Incident – as if she was proud of them. Then she told Dad how Bonnie had saved the champions' trophies and the mayor's chain at the dog show, and as Mum talked Harry interrupted with details she'd forgotten, and then Dad cut in with questions, and soon they all seemed to be talking at once.

Excited by their chatter Bonnie woke up, jumped down, ran round and round the room, then grabbed Mum's slipper from the corner by the fireplace and attacked it. The more they all laughed, the fiercer Bonnie got – and the fiercer Bonnie got, the more they laughed. Together.

It was the Bonnie effect.

The original plan for the day had been that Harry would take his dad for a walk and then the two of them would go to the local burger place for lunch. When Mum had suggested this, Harry had murmured that Dad wouldn't like it, because he was a great cook who liked proper food and hated burgers unless he made them himself. Mum had muttered words to the effect of "Too bad!" So now Harry was amazed to hear her suggest that they all had lunch together.

Much later Harry worked out that it was at this point in the day that he started to feel happy. What they ate for lunch didn't matter, nor what they talked about; it was just nice to feel Bonnie on his knee while Mum and Dad chatted in a friendly way about some things that bored him, and other things that didn't – like when they were young. They laughed too. It was great.

After lunch Harry showed Dad the park where they walked Bonnie, and they kicked his new football around. Bonnie stayed at home to keep Mum company, and it felt nice when it was just the two of them again. They walked to his school, so Dad could see it, and Harry told him how all the kids loved it when Bonnie came to pick him up at the gate.

"That's one popular dog," Dad smiled.

"Well … unless you're a missing letter, or a chicken, or a cyclist, or a postman!" he added.

"Yeah, then she's one mean, bad mutt!" said Harry proudly.

They went back home for tea and cake, and Mum and Dad chatted some more about grown-up stuff, and then it was time for Dad to drive back to London.

"We'll get you up on a visit soon," he promised Harry.

"Sure, Dad," Harry said.

It'd be nice when it happened, but right now he was thinking about other things. His parents had relaxed together, so he was relaxed. And tomorrow his new friend Susie was bringing Princess Daisy to visit, and Zena and Zack were coming for tea as well.

Mum had bought lots of party-type food even though it wasn't a proper party, and he felt quite excited. What's more, he had his own mobile phone at last! Things were definitely looking up.

Once Dad had gone, Harry sat down with Bonnie to watch some TV. She felt sleepy in his arms, just like a soft toy, and he looked back over the day, savouring every detail and smiling to himself.

"You know what, Bons?" he whispered. "You're not a bad dog at all. You're wicked!"

BONNIE thought how easy it was to change things. When that new man came to the door, she could sense – from her coal-black nose to the tip of her silky-white tail – how Harry and his mum were feeling. When your pack were unhappy it was just like when you picked up a little brown pebble thinking it was a chocolate drop. Scrunch-crunch-*crunch* ... then – ow! Painful! Really bad!

Bonnie wished with all her small doggy heart that Harry realized just how well she understood him. Didn't he see her signals? Tail up: good. Tail down: bad. Not very complicated, surely?

She didn't like the way that man made Mum feel at first: tail down! But Bonnie knew a few things about people – if you couldn't make them better, make them laugh; and hey presto, tails up again!

No, there's no such thing as good dog, bad dog, thought Bonnie. All people really need is a happy dog.

Love Bonnie? Then why not read all six of her tail-wagging adventures!

To find out more about the books and the real-life Bonnie who inspired them, visit belmooney.co.uk

Bel Mooney is a well-known journalist and author of many books for adults and children, including the hugely popular Kitty series. She lives in Bath with her husband and real-life Maltese dog, Bonnie, who is the inspiration for this series. Bel says of the real Bonnie: "She makes me laugh and transforms my life with her intelligence, courage and affection. And I just know she's going to pick out a really good card for my birthday."

Find out more about Bel at belmooney.co.uk

Sarah McMenemy is a highly respected artist who illustrates for magazines and newspapers and has worked on diverse commissions all over the world, including art for the London Underground, CD covers and stationery. She illustrated the bestselling City Skylines series and is the creator of the picture books *Waggle* and *Jack's New Boat*. She lives in London.

Find out more about Sarah at sarahmcmenemy.com